Florence Nightingale
Angela Bull

Illustrated by
Karen Heywood

Hamish Hamilton
London

First published 1985 by
Hamish Hamilton Children's Books
27 Wright's Lane, London W8 5TZ
Reprinted 1986
© 1985 text by Angela Bull
© 1985 illustrations by Karen Heywood
All rights reserved

British Library Cataloguing in Publication Data
Bull, Angela
Florence Nightingale. – (Profiles)
1. Nightingale, Florence – Juvenile literature
I. Title   II. Heywood, Karen   III. Series
610.73′092′4   RT37.N5

ISBN 0-241-11477-2

Typeset by Pioneer
Printed in Great Britain at the
University Press, Cambridge

Contents

1 The Younger Daughter

When William and Fanny Nightingale named their baby daughter Florence, after the Italian city where she was born, they had no idea that they were starting a trend. Later, thousands of girls were called Florence, in honour of Florence Nightingale, but in 1820 the choice was very strange. It was like calling a modern baby Majorca or Ibiza.

'How like Fanny!' Mrs Nightingale's friends and relations probably remarked. Fanny was strong-willed, self-confident, and eager to be a leader of fashion. She dreamed of a future as the mistress of a large elegant house, entertaining parties of celebrities. She was beautiful, with sparkling dark eyes, and long romantic curls. She wore expensive clothes. People liked and admired her — and usually forgot to notice the layer of selfishness beneath her charm and good humour.

She was still on an extended honeymoon when Florence was born, on 12 May 1820. After their wedding the Nightingales set off for Italy, and there they lingered for four years. Florence was not their first child. She had an elder sister, Parthenope, born in Naples a year earlier.

Such a long honeymoon was possible because William

Nightingale was very rich. He had inherited a fortune from an uncle, and so he never needed to earn his living. He was six years younger than Fanny, and he trailed about in her shadow, always pleasant and agreeable, but idle and lacking in purpose. Fanny ruled the household.

In 1821 she decided it was time to come home. But where were they to live? William had already built himself a rambling, picturesque house called Lea Hurst, on the land in Derbyshire which he had inherited. Here, he supposed, he and Fanny and their daughters would settle down.

Fanny met the suggestion with cries of horror. Lea Hurst was much too far from London, and it only had fifteen bedrooms. With the family, the maids and footmen, the cook, William's valet, and the children's nurse to accommodate, there was no room for the crowd of fashionable guests she longed to invite. They needed, she told William, something much grander.

Four years of searching led her finally to Embley Park in Hampshire: a large, stately house, with all the drawing-rooms, bedrooms and terraces Fanny wanted. It was near London, and near Fanny's married sisters and their families. Lea Hurst, she announced, could be kept for summer holidays. Embley Park would be their real home.

The two little girls, Parthe and Flo as they were usually called, were now six and five. Fanny, who adored small children, planned a delightful and luxurious life for them. They wore pretty clothes — embroidered muslin dresses with frilled pantalettes

10

William Nightingale

peeping from below the skirts. They had ponies, puppies and kittens, dolls to look after and cousins to play with. Their nurse, Mrs Gale, was kind. Their father took them for walks, and told them jokes and riddles. They were attractive children too, which pleased Fanny; especially Flo, who was slim and graceful, with golden-brown hair cut short, and large dreamy eyes.

Dreamy — that was the trouble. Everything possible was done to promote their happiness, and yet, as she watched her daughters, Fanny noticed, with irritation, that Flo was seldom really happy. She was not grateful for the good things that surrounded her. Often she did not even seem to notice them. Instead she withdrew into a strange world of her own, from which her parents and sister were excluded.

Florence had an intensely vivid imagination. Such a gift should have brought great happiness, but at first it worked the wrong way. Her early years were darkened by the belief that she was really a monster. What kind of a monster exactly, perhaps she could not have said; but it seemed to her that somehow she was terrible, and other people were not. No-one, she thought, had guessed her appalling secret, but they would unless she was very careful. Ignoring her dolls, and the kitten on the hearthrug, she would huddle in a corner of the nursery, trembling in case she betrayed herself at dinner by doing something extraordinary with her knife and fork.

Gradually she realized that she need not be the victim of her imagination; she could be the mistress. By strength of will she banished the monster, and plunged into day-dreams of which she was now the heroine. But the inward struggles and imaginings which absorbed her, had one serious consequence. They meant that she neglected Parthe.

Poor Parthe. Being Flo's elder sister was hard. Compared with Flo, she felt plain and ordinary. Her hair was mousy; Flo's was bright. Her mouth was small and pursed; Flo's was wider, more generous. Parthe's usual expression was plaintive; Flo looked interesting. People noticed her, and were drawn by her strange magnetism.

Parthe was drawn too. She both loved and hated Flo. She longed to be her close companion, but Flo did not need companionship. She wanted to be left alone, and so there were quarrels.

Until the girls were thirteen and twelve a governess

Fanny Nightingale

taught them. Then William took over their education. Every morning they were summoned to the library of Embley Park, where their father stood like a stork behind his high desk. He was so tall that he could never fit himself comfortably into a chair. He mapped out a demanding course of studies for the girls, with French, German, Italian, Latin, Greek, history and philosophy.

Because Flo loved the lessons with their father, Parthe tried hard to enjoy them too; but it was no use. Flo was so much more intelligent than Parthe. She revelled in the difficulties which languages and philosophy provided. Resentment smouldered in Parthe. When she was sixteen, she persuaded Fanny to let her give up lessons, and she arranged flowers and entertained visitors with her mother. Presently she went to stay alone with relations in London, and wrote home to her father, complaining that he seemed to prefer Flo. William replied airily. He could not hide the fact that he felt much closer to his clever younger daughter.

Fanny had ten brothers and sisters. Most had married, so that besides aunts and uncles, the Nightingale girls had twenty-seven first cousins. Parthe felt at home amongst them. In spite of being rich, they were mostly quite ordinary people. They liked clothes and children, going visiting and giving parties. It irritated Parthe that Flo should be so different from them.

Quite how different Flo was, nobody yet realized.

2   Dancing and Mathematics

Through the years of her lessons with William, Flo lived in a world of her own. She was an incurable dreamer. The events of Embley Park passed her by. They were unimportant compared with events in the stories she told herself, just as Parthe was unimportant compared with her day-dream characters.

This powerful inner life, which nobody in the family really knew about, prepared Florence for a strange experience which happened to her when she was sixteen. She wrote afterwards, 'On February 7th, 1837, God spoke to me, and called me to his service.' How it happened, or where she was at the time, she did not record. There was no need to. The details were branded on her memory, as was the certainty that this was not just another day-dream. She had actually heard a voice, outside herself, promising that one day she would be needed for a very special task.

Florence did not tell her family. Fanny and Parthe, who were thrown into hysterics by anything out of the ordinary, would have made a terrible fuss. William would have shrunk from anything that sounded even faintly melodramatic. So the call from God remained another of Florence's secrets.

Embley Park

At about this time Fanny decided that Florence's education should finish. She wanted to bring out her daughters into grown-up society. She meant to present them at Court, and entertain lavishly for them. But, as she pondered her plans, she realized with a shock that Embley Park was not going to be big enough. It needed new kitchens, and at least six more bedrooms. She consulted William, who agreed with her; and he agreed too with Fanny's suggestion that, while their house was altered, they should take the girls on a long tour of Europe. On 8 September 1837 the Nightingales, with a retinue of servants, set off for France, in a coach drawn by six horses.

For teenage Florence the eighteen months spent on the continent were full of excitement and happiness. She became, for once, just the daughter Fanny wanted. The Nightingales made long stays in several European cities, and in each they enjoyed an extravagant social life. Flo banished the musings and day-dreams which had haunted her. She was tall and slim now, with golden-brown hair framing a beautiful oval face, and it was intoxicating to discover how much attention she attracted. At balls she became quite confused amongst all the young men who clamoured to dance with her.

When there were no dances, the Nightingales spent their evenings at the opera. Flo loved music, and the operatic stories appealed to the romantic side of her nature, as the Italian landscape did. But as well, in her spare time, she drew up lists of facts and figures about all the performances she had seen. For the first, but by no means the last time in her life, she turned her enthusiasm into statistics.

The Nightingales returned to England in April 1839. Embley Park was not yet ready, but Fanny did not mind. She had decided to spend the fashionable months from April to July in London. She and her sister, Mrs Nicholson, took a whole floor of the Carlton Hotel, and launched Parthe and Florence, and their Nicholson cousins, into another brilliant social whirl. Wearing white Parisian dresses, they were taken to Buckingham Palace and presented to Queen Victoria, who was less than a year older than Florence.

Florence made an intimate friend of her cousin Marianne Nicholson. They gossiped, sang, and tried on dresses together in their rooms at the Carlton Hotel. Hovering round, ready to applaud the music or escort the girls to balls, was Marianne's brother, Henry. Before long he had fallen in love with Florence.

Fanny watched, delighted that her difficult daughter should have changed, as if by magic, into a charming young lady who was invited everywhere. Soon, no doubt, she would marry, and live happily ever after.

A nasty surprise awaited her. The odd, solitary girl who had dreamed through the years at Embley Park, had been submerged in the whirl of gaiety, but not lost for ever. Now, with invitations arriving by the dozen, and an adoring Henry at her feet, the old personality reasserted itself, and Florence began to rebel. She hated balls and new dresses and flowery valentines. There was a serious side to life, and she had allowed herself to forget it. Above all there had been her call from God. She still did not know why he had called her, and, instead of trying to find out, she had wasted her time on pleasure. She felt sick with guilt at her own unworthiness.

She needed a new purpose in life, and she fixed on mathematics. The opera statistics seemed her only valuable achievement since she gave up lessons with William. She would settle down at home, and study mathematics properly. When she had steadied her

Florence and Parthe

mind, God might speak to her again.

And so began a long struggle with Fanny; for Fanny, of course, was horrified. A girl who was known to enjoy mathematics would lose all her suitors. She would frighten off Henry, and Richard Monckton Milnes, another wealthy gentleman who had fallen in love with her.

Florence's only encouragement came from Aunt Mai, William's sister. William's relatives were always more sympathetic to learning than Fanny's. Aunt Mai asked Florence to stay, got up with her at six o'clock to work, and begged Fanny to let Florence have maths lessons. 'I don't think you have any idea of half that is in her,' she told Fanny.

Fanny did not know, and she did not wish to know. She summoned Florence back to Embley Park, which was ready at last for Fanny's huge house parties. Relentlessly the gaiety went on, and there was no time for study. Florence felt torn in two. She enjoyed her popularity — she could not help it; but at the same time she felt unbearably guilty at frittering her life away on the wrong things.

Tossed to and fro between dancing and mathematics, she was on the edge of a breakdown. Only by losing herself in day-dreams could she forget her problem. What was she to do with herself? What did God want her to do?

3 The Long Conflict

Every summer the Nightingales travelled north to their Derbyshire home, Lea Hurst. Set amongst moors and rocky hills, it was very different from elegant Embley Park.

In the cottages nearby lived many desperately poor people. England, in the 1840s, was going through a time of poverty, unemployment, and even starvation. On her walks Florence found herself drawn to the cottages, longing to help their inhabitants whose lives contrasted so pitifully with her own. She had a new and wonderful sense of being useful as she took them food, clothes and medicines. It was miserable returning to Embley Park at the end of September.

Her experiences in the cottages gave Florence the first clue towards solving the mystery of her vocation. Others followed fast. She spent a few weeks looking after an orphaned baby, though Fanny fretted over the parties she was missing. She nursed her grandmother through a serious illness; and she was with her old nurse, Mrs Gale, when she died. Gradually the truth dawned on her. This was what she was meant to do. God had called her to care for the sick.

If caring for the sick had meant sitting by the bed of

some friend or relation, smoothing pillows and offering hot drinks, Fanny might not have minded too much. But Florence was far too intelligent to be satisfied with that. She wanted to make a proper career of it, to study diseases with their symptoms and cures, to learn to handle birth and death with confidence and efficiency, and to help with operations, which in those days were performed without anaesthetics. In fact, she needed training; but that meant going into a hospital, and early Victorian hospitals were places of squalor and degradation.

They smelled disgusting. Usually there was no adequate drainage, and no idea of cleanliness. There were no bathrooms or lavatories. The beds were seldom changed, so that patient after patient shared the same filthy sheets. No one realized that fresh air was healthy, and windows were frequently boarded up in winter while germs multiplied in the foul, stuffy atmosphere.

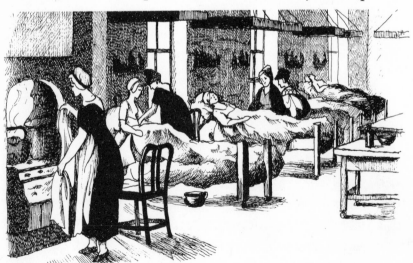

A Victorian hospital

If workmen were called in to whitewash the wards they often became seriously ill, so it was no wonder that most patients died. There were no drugs to relieve pain. Sick people stupefied themselves with gin and brandy, and the police sometimes had to be fetched to quell drunken riots. In these conditions it was so hard to find nurses, that hospitals employed any women who applied, however rough and sluttish they were.

Yet, to work in a hospital was Florence's goal. She had no idea how she would achieve it. Young ladies of her social class never even had careers, let alone careers as nurses. Months, years, passed with their endless round of parties, while she tried to work out what she should do. Her one firm decision was to refuse an offer of marriage from Henry Nicholson. She knew she could not fulfill her vocation if she was a married woman, but Henry was heartbroken, Fanny was furious, and Marianne ended her friendship with Florence.

The only connection Florence had with the medical world was through a friend of her parents, Dr Fowler, the senior physician at Salisbury Infirmary. When, in 1845, the Nightingales asked him to stay, Florence screwed up her courage, and begged to train at his hospital.

There was uproar at Embley Park. No one had previously known of Florence's intention. William was disgusted, Parthe hysterical. Fanny, beside herself with rage, accused Florence of having a love affair with a doctor. There was no discussion of the idea at all, and Dr Fowler hurried away in embarrassment.

But at least the truth was out. The family now knew

Florence's aim. It was far worse than studying mathematics. This would bring real disgrace, for how could Fanny and Parthe ever hold up their heads in society again if people knew that Florence was a nurse?

The conflict rumbled on for nearly ten years. An unmarried daughter had no rights, however old she was — and Florence was now twenty-five. She had to obey her parents. And Florence would not escape through marriage, although she had a second chance when Richard Monckton Milnes proposed to her. Somehow she clung to her calling through storm after storm. Fanny was merciless. She forced Florence to keep up her social engagements, when it was apparent to everyone else that she was ill with the strain.

Parthe was as cruel as Fanny. Her life so far had not been a great success. She had attracted few admirers, and no proposals; but, because she was Florence's sister, enough friends and invitations had come her way to satisfy her vanity. The thought of being left to manage on her own, while Florence followed a discreditable career, and people sneered at the Nightingales behind their backs, renewed all Parthe's girlhood resentments. When friends rescued Florence by taking her abroad, Parthe insisted on having her undivided companionship for six months on her return. Six months of Parthe's bitterness destroyed all the good effects of Florence's holiday.

Most women would have cracked completely under such pressure. Florence almost did — but not quite. Somehow, in secret, she kept her vocation alive. Long after she got home from the parties, which now seemed

Kaiserwerth

so dreary, her bedroom candle burned as she read health surveys and hospital reports. When she travelled, she managed to inspect foreign hospitals. Once when the Nightingales were in Germany for the sake of Parthe's health — undermined, like Florence's, in the struggle — and Florence revealed that she was going to visit the hospital at Kaiserwerth, Parthe screamed and flung her bracelets at Florence; but Florence went.

Kaiserwerth interested her particularly. Its nurses were not sluts off the streets, but women bound by religious vows, like nuns. They proved that nurses could command respect.

But by now the opposition was fading. William, distressed by Fanny's and Parthe's behaviour, had at last taken Florence's side. Other friends gathered to help her. Two of them, Sidney and Elizabeth Herbert, who were rich and aristocratic enough to please Fanny, spread the news round London that Florence Nightingale was England's leading expert in health matters.

Florence was thirty-two when Elizabeth Herbert finally launched her career. The Institution for the Care of Sick Gentlewomen in Distressed Circumstances was opening a nursing home in London. Elizabeth told the management committee that Florence would be the best person to take charge of it. Once again Fanny and Parthe raged, but now their cries were like waves beating helplessly on a rock. Florence accepted the position.

Exhausting though it was, the long fight with her family had its value. It changed Florence from a charming girl into an iron lady; and, within two years, an iron lady was what she needed to be.

4   The Call Comes

For years Florence had dreamed of having a hospital of her own. When a friend once admired the elegance of Embley Park, Florence replied that whenever she looked at the rows of windows, she thought about how she would turn it into a hospital, and where she would put the beds.

Now, at last, she had a nursing home to organize; everything, from the operations to the ordering of jam for breakfast, interested her. Some of her ideas, like a lift to take hot food quickly up several floors, were startlingly new, but Florence was determined that her patients should be warm, well-fed and comfortable. Each one, if she could manage it, would go home cured. The patients were astonished by the good food, clean sheets, and vases of flowers. They had never heard of a hospital like it; and when they left, they wrote to Florence with overflowing gratitude. 'Thank you, thank you, darling Miss Nightingale,' one typical letter began.

When all was running smoothly, Florence began to look outwards again. Once more she visited hospitals and collected statistics; once more she pondered on how to attract better nurses. The actual business of nursing still fascinated her. She did as much as she could in the nursing home; and during an epidemic of cholera — a violent form of stomach upset, which swept through undrained slum streets in hot weather — she took charge of the cholera wards in a big London hospital. Fanny and Parthe sent hysterical notes, imploring her to find more suitable work, but Florence took no notice. She was too happy to be worried by her tiresome relations.

Florence ran her nursing home from the summer of 1853 to the late autumn of 1854. Short though the time was, it gave her just enough experience to face with confidence the tremendous challenge which was suddenly thrown down for her. But perhaps the confidence did not only come from her seventeen months of practical nursing. Since God had called her, all those years ago, she had been waiting for her special task; sure now that, when the moment came, she would not fail.

The call came in November 1854. The task she was offered was simple, yet enormous. She was asked to go to Turkey, to an unknown place named Scutari, and nurse British soldiers, the casualties of a war being fought on a little peninsula sticking into the Black Sea, called the Crimea.

The Crimean War had begun in March 1854, when Britain and France declared war on Russia. Their reasons for doing so were not particularly honourable. The Czar, the ruler of Russia, had constructed a huge naval base at Sebastopol in the Crimea, and gathered his warships there to threaten an old enemy, Turkey.

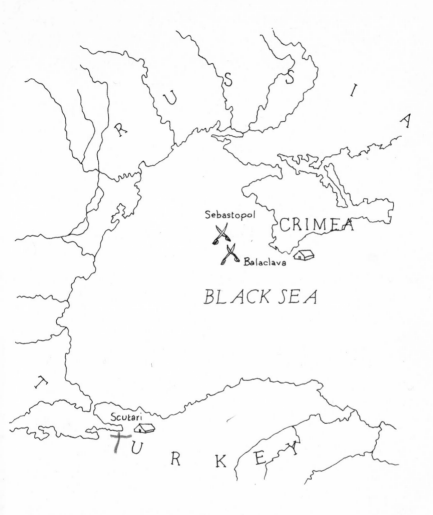

The British Government considered it was Britain's right to rule the seas, and they hated the thought of a Russian fleet so near the Mediterranean. In November 1853 a Russian victory in a sea battle against Turkey was the last straw. Britain and France declared war on the pretence of defending Turkey, but really to smash the Russians.

The war was disastrous. The British soldiers were brave enough, and won battles at Alma and Balaclava through their own good luck and determination, and through the Russians' feebleness. But the British generals were hopeless. Britain had been at peace for forty years, and no one had any idea how to run a war. The shortages of equipment were criminal. The army lacked food, bedding, tents, clothes and medical supplies. Soon the soldiers began to succumb, not just to the inevitable wounds of war, but to all kinds of diseases that preyed on their weakened state — especially cholera. By the autumn of 1854, the cholera victims outnumbered the battle casualties.

The generals tried to hush things up, but they were prevented by a clever newspaper man, William Howard Russell. He had gone to the Crimea to report for *The Times*, and he was soon sending home a flow of sensational articles.

By now the army had reached their goal, the naval base at Sebastopol, and had dug themselves into trenches to besiege it. The British public, lulled into the belief that everything was going rather well, were shocked when Russell's reports about the real situation began to appear. He revealed that the soldiers were living on half a pound of mouldy biscuit and half a pound of salt pork a day, and that was all; that no hot drinks could be provided as the coffee beans were raw, and anyway there was no fuel to make fires; that the camps had been churned up into bogs, and that men were sleeping on blankets in the mud; and that when they became ill, or were wounded, there were hardly

Sidney Herbert

any doctors, and no nurses to attend to them. They were crammed into hospital ships, with little regard for their comfort, and transported across the Black Sea to the Barrack Hospital at Scutari, where many of them died.

It was a fortunate chance that Sidney Herbert, the friend who had already encouraged Florence, now held a government post as Secretary at War. He was responsible for the well-being of the soldiers. Horrified by the articles in *The Times*, he dashed off a letter to Florence. Could she possibly collect a party of nurses, he asked, and go out to the Crimea to care for the sick and wounded. Everything she needed to improve medical conditions would be paid for.

Florence too had read *The Times*. As Sidney wrote to her, she was writing to him, putting herself at his disposal. Sidney Herbert simply wanted the suffering of the troops to be relieved. Florence had a second motive. If her nurses played their part well before the public gaze — and all eyes would certainly be on Scutari — they might win for their profession the status it lacked.

But first the nurses had to be chosen, and that was difficult. Sidney was prepared to allow forty, if forty could be found. Florence advertised, and waited. She was disappointed. The nurses who applied were mostly old and inefficient, failures snatching at the chance of good pay. Only fourteen of them were worth engaging. Florence turned to the Roman Catholic and Anglican nuns who worked in the slums of some big cities. They had experience of cholera epidemics, and most were better educated and more practical than the nurses. Selecting some of them, Florence was able to bring her numbers up to thirty-eight. That would have to do.

To bind the thirty-eight women together, Florence made rules for them. They would all be equal, and they would all obey her. They would share the same food and accommodation. The nuns could wear their habits, but the nurses would wear identical grey dresses and white caps. They would all earn twelve shillings (60p) a week.

When the appointment of Florence and her nurses was announced in the newspapers, there was great interest. It was unknown for a woman to be given such an important job. Florence was a centre of attention. Everyone was talking about her, and Fanny and Parthe were thrilled. Forgetting how they had opposed her, they rushed to London to help with the packing, and to receive the compliments and good wishes intended for Florence.

Florence was too busy drawing up lists of equipment to notice them. Sidney Herbert had assured her that she would find that medical supplies had been delivered to Scutari by the time she arrived, but Florence did not believe him. Luckily *The Times* had given her the fund of money raised by its readers in response to William Russell's articles. Florence was planning to buy everything she might need on her way to Turkey.

5 In the Barrack Hospital

As the boat steamed up the Bosphorus, on the last stage
of the journey to Turkey, Florence was in her most
practical mood. She had equipped herself with food
and medicines as she crossed France, and she felt ready
for whatever difficulties lay ahead.

The other nurses were excited and impatient. Few of
them had travelled before; and they gazed first
westwards at the domes and spires of Constantinople,
and the camels swaying along the coastal roads, and
then eastwards at the massive Barrack Hospital, on a
rise above the sea.

'Oh, Miss Nightingale,' one exclaimed, 'when we
arrive, let us get straight to nursing the poor fellows.'

'The strongest will be wanted at the wash-tubs,'
Florence replied.

Her knowledge of hospitals led her to expect dirt,
but even she was unprepared for the filthiness of the
Barrack Hospital at Scutari. To call it a hospital at all
was a mockery. It was a hell-hole of disease and dirt.

From the once splendid, but now crumbling,
quadrangle, spiked with minarets, drifted a disgusting
smell of human refuse. Inside, packed together, lay
thousands of soldiers, ill, wounded and dying. Their

clothes and blankets were stiff with blood, and crawling with lice. There was no water for washing, and all the drains were blocked. Almost every man had diarrhoea, but there were neither medicines nor special diets to relieve it. Even those in agonies of stomach ache had only undercooked lumps of meat to eat, or the greasy water it was boiled in.

The blame for this terrible situation rested between the War Office in London, who had never thought through the problems of equipping an army for Turkey, and the army itself, with its foolishly rigid regulations. If, for example, new shirts were urgently needed for men who had lost all their clothes, a request was passed through a long chain of officials until it reached an office called the Commissariat. The Commissariat staff checked, found no shirts, wrote 'none in stock' on the form, and that was the end of the matter. It was nobody's job to ask for more. And the

Scutari Barracks

shortage of shirts was only one of hundreds of shortages. It was fortunate that Florence had not believed Sidney Herbert about the supplies, for Scutari Hospital had nothing.

Overwhelmed by their difficulties, the doctors let things slide. How could they cope, with no drugs, no dressings, and no invalid food? They dealt with injured limbs by amputating them, without anaesthetics, and without even a screen to hide the victim's agony from his companions. Soldiers were expected to be tough. They had to be.

Florence and her nurses were unaware of all this as they disembarked at Scutari's rickety landing stage, and climbed the muddy slope to the hospital. They knew they were needed, and they anticipated an enthusiastic welcome. Instead, they were met with hostility. The doctors had heard that a rich young lady was coming, and they were not pleased. The army was a man's world. Nobody wanted women fussing about, and getting in the way. Besides it seemed that, by sending nurses, the War Office was criticizing the hospital; and criticism made the doctors very indignant. They showed their disapproval by allotting Florence and her thirty-eight nurses just six, tiny, dirty rooms, one with a corpse lying in it. There was neither food, furniture nor lighting for them. After Florence had contrived mugs of milkless tea, the nurses went to bed on bare wooden divans, while rats scuttled round them.

Next morning it was made clear that the doctors did not want the nurses in the wards. All the nurses were

Girls making lint

shocked and dismayed — except Florence. She was
used to opposition, and she had triumphed over it
before. She calmed the nurses, and found useful jobs
for them. Some checked the stores they had brought,
some tore up old linen for bandages, some — including
Florence — began cooking invalid meals.

Florence knew the diet that cholera patients needed.
She made huge milk puddings from arrowroot she had
bought in France, laced them with wine, and offered
them to the doctors. Cooking was something the doctors
could approve. They accepted the puddings.

This state of affairs lasted for a week. It was hard on
the nurses. They had come to help, and all around
them soldiers lay suffering and dying for want of care.
But Florence waited patiently. She knew that if the
nurses went into the wards before the doctors invited
them, there would be trouble. They might be thrown

out altogether. If they proved their self-control by waiting, the doctors might, in the end, send for them.

The breakthrough came at last. On 5 November there was a battle at Inkerman, outside Sebastopol. The British won, but their casualties were enormous. At the same time the weather changed for the worse. Icy winds swept over the camps. With no tents, no fires, and no proper food to sustain them, the soldiers collapsed in their thousands.

Boat after boat transported them to Scutari. The hospital was already overcrowded, but still patients were carried in, and squeezed into every inch of space, along the corridors and up the staircases. Suddenly there was panic among the doctors. They imagined the whole hospital turning into a vast morgue, and themselves dying among the cholera victims. And at last they remembered the rich young lady cooking the arrowroot puddings. She looked so calm and steady, with her smooth hair and gentle manners.

Someone hurried to Florence's little room with the longed-for request. Things were desperate, he said. Could she and her nurses come and help?

They were ready, and they knew exactly what to do. While the nurses sewed up cotton bags stuffed with straw, so that the men would at least have clean mattresses to lie on, Florence toured the hospital, making notes of all that was needed.

She had seen terrible hospitals before, but nowhere like Scutari. 'I have seen Hell,' she said of it afterwards. She was not just a practical person; she was a woman of imagination and sensitivity. The sights, sounds and smells appalled her. They were branded for ever on her memory, but they spurred her to action too. She had the money raised by *The Times*, and unlimited funds promised by Sidney Herbert. Immediately she began spending it. She sent to Constantinople for clothes, food, china, cutlery, soap, baths, bed-pans, operating tables — the list was endless. Rapidly, and by herself, she stocked the whole hospital.

The task of cleaning was urgent too. Florence knew, as many doctors did not, that dirt was fatal to health. She engaged two hundred local men to unblock the drains and lavatories. She had the floors scrubbed for the first time anyone could remember, and she organized the soldiers' wives to wash clothes and bedding.

Meanwhile the nurses were doing their proper work at last. Under Florence's supervision they gave out medicines and dressed wounds. Florence bought a screen to shield patients during operations, and she stood beside them all through the ordeal, encouraging them by her presence to endure the agony.

Conditions gradually began to change. Formerly for a sick or wounded man to be moved from Sebastopol to Scutari made little difference. Neglect, suffering and death were the rule in both places. Now, as the soldiers were carried off the hospital ships, and into the Barrack Hospital, they could hardly believe their eyes. Clean clothes and clean beds awaited them, water to wash in, hot nourishing food, and nurses to treat them. Florence had called Scutari Hell, but the men thought differently.

'We felt we were in Heaven,' one said.

6 The Lady with the Lamp

Two months at Scutari gave Florence more authority
than any Englishwoman had ever achieved before,
except a queen. Women had never been powerful in
Britain. They could not be members of Parliament,
judges or civil servants. The first woman doctor,
Elizabeth Blackwell, had just qualified, but she had
studied in America and Switzerland as British univer-
sities were for men only. No woman had ever taken
charge of a huge institution like a military hospital.

Florence attended to every detail, as she had done in
her nursing home. Still patients flooded in — four
thousand arrived in just seventeen days in December
— and Florence had a derelict wing of the hospital
repaired at lightning speed to accommodate them. As
well as cholera, there was now scurvy, a disease caused
by lack of fresh vegetables. Shiploads of cabbages had
been sent from England, but they had rotted before
they reached the troops, and been dumped in the sea,
where all the rubbish, from rags to corpses, washed up
and down.

With new standards of cleanliness and comfort,
Florence hoped the death rate would fall, but at first it
went on rising. She faced the problem with typical

Alexis Soyer

determination and intelligence. Unlike most doctors, she had actually given a good deal of thought to the causes of disease and death, and now she suspected that the water supply might be contaminated. She got workmen to investigate, and they discovered the dead body of a horse in the pipe through which all the hospital water flowed. As its remains were carted away, the worst source of infection and death was removed.

The food improved amazingly. Alexis Soyer, the French chef from a London club, arrived unexpectedly to take charge of the kitchens. Under his supervision, the meals became tasty and nourishing, with fresh bread, soups and roasts instead of lumps of boiled meat. Whenever Soyer visited a ward, he was greeted with cheers.

But the heroine of the hospital was undoubtedly Florence, and she was not just loved for the improvements she made. Throughout the war the soldiers had been treated with less consideration than animals. Starving and frozen, they had been abandoned, by officers and doctors alike, to die in their own blood and filth. At the Barrack Hospital they found someone who cared for them as individuals, and they responded with a gratitude that flowered into adoration.

Florence was often on her feet for twenty-four hours together. She moved from bed to bed, dressing wounds and relieving pain. She made a rule that no one should die alone. Either she would sit by the bedside, or, if she

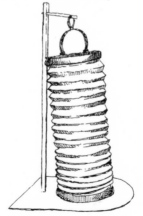

Turkish lamp used by Florence

was called away, another nurse would take her place. Every night she made a last round of the wards, a quiet figure in a black dress and shawl, and a white cap, carrying a little Turkish lamp. The soldiers gave her the name of 'the lady with the lamp'.

'What a comfort it was to see her pass even', one soldier wrote. 'She would speak to one, and nod and smile to many more. She could not do it to all, you know. We lay there by hundreds. But we could kiss her shadow as it fell.'

Not only did she nurse the patients, and oversee every detail of the hospital; Florence also found time to write voluminous letters to Sidney Herbert in London, telling him all that had been done, and all that needed to be done. The Turkish winter was bitterly cold. The ink froze in its pot as, after her final round of the wards, Florence sat wrapped in shawls, writing and writing, driven on by anger and concern. Never again must a hell like Scutari be permitted. The army *must* re-organize its medical services, she wrote. It *must* provide better food and equipment, and better means of getting them to the troops. Records *must* be kept of how many soldiers had died, and why. A study of statistics might prevent another calamity.

Her letters were passed on to Queen Victoria, who was appalled to learn of the plight of her soldiers. She wrote to Sidney Herbert — 'I wish Miss Nightingale and the ladies would tell these poor noble wounded and sick men that *no-one* takes a warmer interest, or feels more for their suffering, or admires their courage and heroism *more* than their queen.' Her message was

In the hospital

read aloud to the astonished soldiers, and pinned up in the wards. Never before had a monarch written such words to ordinary troops. Another letter came for Florence herself. The queen, it said, had observed Florence's 'goodness and self-devotion with the highest approval and admiration.'

Unfortunately the love and praise showered on Florence provoked envy and resentment. At her suggestion, Sidney Herbert sent out a committee from England to examine conditions in the camps and hospitals, and its report was fiercely critical of the army's medical men. They got their revenge by obstructing many of Florence's plans. She might look serene as she toured the wards with her lamp, but presently her serenity hid a mass of niggling problems and worries.

There were difficulties with the nurses too. They, like Florence, were under great strain, and most did not have her inner strength to cope with it. Some disliked taking her orders; some disagreed with her over the treatment of particular cases; some bickered amongst themselves. One objected strongly to the uniform. 'If I'd known, ma'am, about the caps,' she told Florence, 'I wouldn't have come.' Some nurses, like the nuns from Bermondsey, were heroic in what they did, but on the whole they were a disappointment, never fulfilling Florence's hopes.

By April 1855 the Barrack Hospital was running smoothly, and Florence began to look outwards. Two additional military hospitals had been established on the actual Crimean peninsula, and there were complaints about them both. Florence decided to investigate.

She sailed from Scutari to Balaclava, a seaport beneath the heights of Sebastopol, and set out on horseback for the hospitals. Their state of dirt and inefficiency reminded her all too painfully of how the Barrack Hospital had been. The nurses were rude; the doctors unco-operative. Florence began drawing up plans for re-organization, but suddenly it was all too much. In the middle of a trying interview with the nursing superintendent, she fainted; and, as people gathered round, they realized that she was burning with fever.

Exhaustion, and months of exposure to infection, had at last overcome even Florence. For a fortnight she lay on the brink of death, in a hospital outside Balaclava. Dismay spread among the troops, and soldiers in Scutari wept at the news.

The devoted care of one of her best nurses saved her life, but only just. Thin, pale, and with her hair cut short to keep her fevered head cool, Florence was a shadow of her old self. She returned to Scutari, and found many of her arrangements muddled. The chaos of the Balaclava hospitals fretted her. Aunt Mai, who had taken her side over mathematics long ago, came to stay, and was horrified to find her frail, weary niece, struggling with endless problems.

Compared with her early time of success, Florence's last months at Scutari were dark. Illness dogged her, the doctors still opposed her; only the soldiers loved her. And gradually the cause of these suffering men quite replaced the cause of nursing in Florence's mind. The nurses had let her down with their quarrels and selfishness, but she felt she could never do enough for the brave, loyal and uncomplaining soldiers.

Into her overcrowded life she fitted extra work for them. She wrote their letters — for many could not write, banked their money, and opened recreation rooms for convalescents. 'Spoiling the brutes', the military commander at Scutari growled, but Florence did not listen. The men, she believed, must be repaid for all the misery the army had inflicted upon them.

That was her chief feeling when, on 29 April 1856, peace was declared. The human cost of a pointless war had been too great. 'And' she wrote pessimistically, 'in six months all these sufferings will be forgotten.'

7 Homecoming

As letters were sent from Scutari to England, and convalescent soldiers returned home, the legend of Florence Nightingale, the lady with the lamp, steadily grew. She had won the hearts of ordinary people, as no other woman had ever done. Pamphlets about her work at the Barrack Hospital were put on sale for a penny, and snapped up instantly. Pictures of her were circulated, both imaginary portraits, and drawings of a nightingale, with Florence's head and white cap, perching by the bedside of a soldier. China figures were made of her, and Madame Tussaud put on a waxwork display called 'Miss Nightingale administering to the Sick and Wounded.' Songs were composed about her, and sung in concerts and music halls. Some typical lines ran —

The wounded they love her as it has been seen,
She's the soldiers' preserver, they call her their queen.
May God give her strength, and her heart never fail,
One of Heaven's best gifts is Miss Nightingale.

Queen Victoria showed her admiration by sending Florence a brooch, specially designed by Prince Albert.

The words 'Blessed are the merciful' were inscribed on a gold frame encircling a cross, with three diamond stars on top.

The feelings of the Nightingale family had changed utterly. There was no question now of Florence disgracing herself by nursing. They basked in her fame. 'We are ducks who have hatched a wild swan,' Fanny told the writer Mrs Gaskell, prepared to be humble herself now that she had a daughter to boast about. When a meeting was called in London to discuss how Florence might best be honoured, Fanny and Parthe refused to go in case they were overcome with emotion; but they held a reception at their London hotel afterwards, to hear all about it, and gloried in the importance of being Nightingales.

Excitement mounted when it was known that the last patient had left the Barrack Hospital, and Florence was coming home. The Government offered to send a warship to fetch her. The Mayors of Dover and Folkestone, ports where she might perhaps land, arranged huge receptions for her. Regimental bands competed for the privilege of playing her ashore.

Florence heard of these preparations with horror. A public triumph was just what she did not want. Worn out physically and emotionally, she was haunted by memories of the thousands who had died in those terrible hospitals. 'Oh my poor men,' she wrote in a private note, 'I am a bad mother to come home and leave you in your Crimean graves.' Her sense of failure far outweighed any feeling of success, and made the idea of rejoicing unbearable.

Brooch presented to Florence by Queen Victoria

Luckily Aunt Mai was still with her, and Aunt Mai's married name was Mrs Smith. Florence seized with thankfulness on the anonymity this offered. There were no passports in those days, so Florence pretended to be Aunt Mai's daughter, and simply called herself Miss Smith. No-one knew what Miss Nightingale looked like, except the doctors and patients at Scutari, and they had gone away. Under her false name it was easy for Florence to travel to England without being recognized.

By now it was July, and her family was staying at Lea Hurst. Preparations for a Derbyshire welcome were well in hand. Florence was to be greeted with bands and processions and arches of flowers. No-one dreamed that she would come home unannounced, so there was nobody waiting at the station when a thin frail lady, dressed in black, climbed down from the train; and no crowds lined the village street as she walked up to Lea

Hurst alone. Only her mother's housekeeper saw Florence's approach from a window, and ran out, in tears, to meet her.

Fanny, Parthe, and even William, had never understood Florence, and they understood less than ever the tense, weary woman who returned from Scutari. Why, they wondered, could she not sit back and enjoy her fame, like any normal person? Parthe was thrilled by the sackfuls of letters that poured in, the gifts and poems and proposals of marriage. Florence hardly looked at them. 'You can answer them,' she told Parthe indifferently. She refused to give interviews, or autographs, or even accept invitations to dinner. 'In no way, I am determined, will I contribute to making a show of myself,' she wrote in a private note.

But very soon a special invitation arrived. Queen Victoria wished for a full account of Florence's experiences, and she asked Florence to visit her at Balmoral. This invitation alone Florence accepted, but it was not for reasons that Fanny and Parthe understood. Florence did not want to talk to the queen about the past. She wanted to talk about the future.

8 Saving the Army

Florence wanted to lay before the queen the plight of ordinary soldiers, and ask for her support in a campaign to improve their health and conditions. Those endless lines of filthy, blood-stained men, moaning for water, or screaming under the surgeons' knives, must not be forgotten now that the war was over. There might be another war, and the same disasters must not occur again. Florence did not mean to put her case in words alone. Working with feverish urgency, she gathered pages of facts and statistics to back her arguments, and took them to Balmoral with her.

The queen and Prince Albert were impressed by her knowledge and concern for the army. 'I wish we had her at the War Office,' the queen remarked. They were impressed too by her incredible lack of interest in her own achievements. Indeed Florence's strange mixture of characteristics surprised everyone who met her at this time; they discovered that she could be both an iron lady and the lady with the lamp.

Outwardly she was almost insignificant — slender, dressed in black, with her hair combed back from her thin, pale face. The glow which had attracted admirers in her youth had quite gone. Yet a few minutes' conversation with her revealed a remarkable strength of will. It was a quality the doctors and nurses at Scutari had always recognized. They might object to her orders, but when she said — 'It must be done' — she had a quiet authority which no one could resist.

And, just as with the doctors and nurses, Florence got her way with the queen. She had decided that what was needed was a Royal Commission, a sort of public inquiry, on the health of the army. The queen heartily agreed. But though the wills of the two women were strong, their power was limited. Florence held no official position. The queen could advise, but she could not dictate. Nevertheless, acting together, and using all their powers of persuasion, they manoeuvred the right Cabinet minister round to their viewpoint. A Royal Commission was set up, with Sidney Herbert as chairman.

Things were at last moving in the direction Florence wanted. Now she might have allowed herself a few pleasures, taken a holiday, even returned to her old career of nursing. Instead, with a speed and obsessive determination which swept aside all minor interests, she began collecting all the information she could find which might be useful to the Royal Commission, and arranging it in graphs, tables and pie charts. (Florence invented the pie chart.)

The amount of work she got through would have exhausted a far stronger person, and since her illness in Balaclava, Florence had never been really well. She ate almost nothing. Sometimes her breathing was

constricted, or her heart thudded unevenly. Her head ached, and in moments of stress she fainted. Yet she worked relentlessly, devouring medical reports, and dashing round London, on foot or in cabs, to visit hospitals and barracks. Wound up by the pressures of Scutari, and of her passionate care for the soldiers, she had lost the ability to unwind.

She had taken rooms in a London hotel, and Fanny and Parthe insisted on joining her. They assured her, and everyone else, that they had come to help; and at first they enjoyed entertaining all the well-known people who came to call, while, in an inner room, Florence sat hunched over her papers. But presently the reflected glory paled. The weather became uncomfortably hot. Everyone who could, left London. Still Florence worked on. Fanny and Parthe grew more and more bored and irritated. They lay about on sofas, grumbling and complaining; yet, as Florence bitterly said, 'convinced of their devotion to another who is dying of overwork.'

It should have been obvious that Florence did not need them. She had a small band of genuine helpers, led by Sidney Herbert, who did not mind how much they did for her. Perhaps Fanny and Parthe were jealous, as they found themselves outside the circle. They punished Florence in mean little ways, like refusing her the use of their carriage, and taking her bedroom for their own guests.

But nothing stopped Florence. Ill though she was, she drove the Royal Commission to its conclusion, and she was rewarded. Everything she wanted was promised, from an army medical school to new drains for barracks. Yet even this did not satisfy her. The promises were merely words on paper. They would have to be put into effect by the War Office, and bitter experience had shown her what the War Office was like. If it had cheated the army in time of war, with its bunglings over shirts and cabbages and medical supplies, it would certainly cheat a Royal Commission. The War Office would have to be reformed.

Commonsense should have warned Florence that this was beyond her powers, but by now she was becoming unbalanced. Her sympathy for suffering soldiers somehow became transformed into a crusade against a vast state institution — for that was what the War Office was. It was a laborious, joyless crusade. Overwork, illness, and troubles with Fanny and Parthe filled Florence with the sense that she alone was fighting the world. Her cause might be noble, but she was ceasing to be noble herself. She became angry, self-pitying, and wildly unreasonable. She was convinced that nobody had ever worked as hard as she did. She believed the effort would kill her, and nobody would care. She watched the people around her with fury. Fanny and Parthe wilted under the strain of arranging the flowers. Sidney went on holiday. She alone was obliged to save the British army.

This was the worst period of Florence's life. Power made her demanding; illness frayed her nerves. Then, as she quarrelled with her family, Parthe saved the situation by getting married! At last an admirer, a wealthy widower called Sir Harry Verney, came her way, and she snapped him up. Fanny was delighted. Suddenly they no longer wished to bother with Florence. They left her alone.

Meanwhile Sidney Herbert, as head of the War Office, had the job of reforming it. Ever since he and his wife had encouraged Florence's nursing, she had relied on him more than anyone. They were close friends. His warmth and charm — for he was a delightful man — softened Florence's harshness. Now, as she gathered facts and figures to help his case, he began to falter. He was ill, he told her. He couldn't go on.

Once Florence had been a dedicated nurse. Now she had lost patience with illness. She raged at Sidney, telling him that her health was far worse than his. She was confined to bed almost all the time, but she never stopped working. He was threatening to throw up a great crusade because his head ached. Remorselessly she drove him on.

But even Florence's will power could not halt the kidney disease which Sidney had contracted. Together the two invalids, one fiercely impatient, one meekly resigned, struggled with their impossible task. Florence expected death for herself almost daily, but it was Sidney who finally collapsed. 'Poor Florence,' he murmured as he was dying, 'our joint work unfinished.'

As another man took his place at the War Office, the plans for reform faded away. They had never, in fact, been necessary, for all the Royal Commission's recommendations were carried through. Barracks were drained and ventilated properly; army food improved; the death rate from disease dropped dramatically. The changes were entirely due to Florence's dynamic combination of intelligence and determination; but, as she mourned for Sidney, she could hardly raise her head from her mountains of paper to see what had happened.

9 A Nurse after all

People who remembered the lady with the lamp, nodding and smiling to the rows of sick soldiers, always patient and gentle, would have found it hard to recognize the irritable invalid, snowed under with piles of paper, who now seldom rose from her bed. The humanity seemed to have gone out of her. She never stopped working for a minute. Because she had won herself the reputation of the foremost expert on medical matters, she was consulted about the building and equipping of hospitals, about nurses for workhouses, and the health of the army in India. She wrote books, and countless letters, full of her theories about everything, from cleanliness and ventilation to the correct design for sinks; but she wrote without pleasure. She was exhausted, resentful, and miserable about Sidney's death. Florence Nightingale in the early 1860s was not a nice person.

The only sign of the old Florence was her love for her cats. There was nearly always a cat or two, coiled round her neck, or sharing the bed with her pens and notebooks. She cherished them, as she had once cherished her patients; and was soothed by their quiet movements.

She knew that her incessant, grinding work was harmful to her, but somehow she could not stop. It was odd that someone who had been an inspired nurse was so poor at looking after herself. Stuck in her groove, her good qualities were nearly obliterated.

Then, slowly, the old self, the self who had loved people more than statistics, began to revive. The first hint of a change came when, after nine years of estrangement, she visited her mother at Embley Park. Fanny was now elderly, and half blind. Gone were the romantic curls and elegant dresses; and, sadly, gone too was the old companionship with Parthe. Lady Verney, as Parthe now was, had little time for her mother.

Florence made conditions. She would go to Embley Park only if she could eat and work in her own room, and see nobody except Fanny. But Fanny's plight touched her, and old barriers began to come down. Next year Florence ventured as far as Lea Hurst, and spent three months with her parents. She enjoyed talking about philosophy with her father again; and Fanny, she admitted, was dearer to her than she had ever been. Her feeble state reminded Florence that once, before statistics claimed her, she had been a nurse.

So as William and Fanny grew older, and less able to cope, Florence took charge of them. Parthe said she was too busy with her social life. Florence, still an invalid herself, added her parents' bills and business letters to her own piles of correspondence. The army and its concerns were slipping away from her. As she

Florence in old age

supervised the nursing of William and Fanny, her thoughts turned to the Nightingale Training School.

At the end of the Crimean War, the soldiers had shown their gratitude to Florence by contributing a day's pay each to a fund which Florence had used to set up a training school for nurses in London. In the early stages she had kept her usual watchful eye on every detail. Then other preoccupations had intervened, and she had almost lost touch.

By 1870 the Nightingale Training School was in serious difficulties. Florence was horrified to discover how chaotic the organization had become, and how the standard of nurses had fallen. The old longing to advance the cause of nursing began to stir in her again. If she could take the school over, she would restore it, as she had restored the hospital at Scutari. The Nightingale nurses would be famous. In the desert of paper and ink, where she had been living for so long, the prospect of returning to her first love was like a glimpse of an oasis.

Bedridden though she was, she took control of the

training school. Standards soared; requests from hospitals for her nurses poured in. Florence chose her students carefully, and devoted herself to them as if they were the daughters she had never had. She did not just train them; she made life pleasant for them. She held tea parties for them, sent them flowers when they were ill, and even paid for their holidays.

Her return to the world of nursing filled her with a peace that was never shaken again. She grew plump, and amazingly placid. William and Fanny died, but she made friends with Parthe and the Verney family. Her affections spread outwards in widening circles. She still had paper and ink by her bed, but she used them to write chatty letters, not graphs and pie charts. She seized every excuse to send people presents.

She reached the age of seventy, then eighty. Queen Victoria died, and the new king, Edward VII, decided that this most legendary of his subjects should receive the award of the Order of Merit. Her impact on the life of the country had been immeasurable. Through her influence hospitals had become clean, wholesome places, and nurses well-trained and caring women. It was impossible to calculate how many lives had been saved because of Florence Nightingale.

She was the first woman to be given the Order of Merit. The king's representative handed it to her in her bright, dainty bedroom. 'Too kind,' Florence murmured, not quite understanding what was happening, 'too kind.'

Those were her last recorded words. On 13 August 1910, at the age of ninety, she died.